No Hitting!
by Karen Katz

Grosset & Dunlap
An Imprint of Penguin Group (USA) Inc.

ISBN 978-0-448-45596-9   10 9 8 7 6 5 4

I'M MAD!
I want to hit my
baby brother.
That's not okay,
but I can . . .

hit some
pots and pans.
**BANG,
BANG,
BANG!**

I'M MAD!
I want to squeeze the cat. That's not okay, but I can . . .

squeeze some clay.

SQUISH,

SQUISH,

SQUISH!

I'M MAD!
I want to jump
up and down and
yell and scream!
That's not okay,
but I can . . .

jump up and down
in the leaves!
CRUNCH,
CRUNCH,
CRUNCH!

I'M MAD!

I want to scribble in my sister's book. That's not okay, but I can . . .

scribble on my
art pad.
SCRIBBLE,
SCRIBBLE,
SCRIBBLE!

I'M MAD!

I want to stick out my tongue at Mommy. That's not okay, but I can . . .

stick out my
tongue and
lick a fruit pop.
SLURP,
SLURP,
SLURP!

Do you feel better now?

YES! I'm not mad anymore!